IYLA
GOES TO
THE DENTIST

WRITTEN BY **DR. BATOOL KAZMI**
ILLUSTRATED BY JUPITERS MUSE

Tellwell Talent
www.tellwell.ca

ISBN
978-0-2288-5473-9 (Hardcover)
978-0-2288-5474-6 (Paperback)

Dedicated to:

Iyla, Armaan, Mataya, Melina, Sophia, Rayyan & Aliza.

With special thanks to my father for always editing my work.

Today is a big day for lyla. She is going to the dentist for the very first time.

Although lyla brushes her teeth every morning and at night, she is a little bit nervous to go to the dentist's office. Her older brother has been there a couple of times. He tells lyla not to worry. "Going to the dentist can be lots of fun," he says.

When lyla gets to the dentist's office, she has to wait in the waiting room. The waiting room has some nice toys to play with and books to read.

Then, Iyla hears a lady call out her name! Dr. Sugarbaum, the dentist, is ready to see her now. Dr. Sugarbaum's dental assistant, Clare, takes Iyla into the operatory. Iyla sees two small chairs and a funny looking big chair.

Dr. Sugarbaum gives lyla a big smile and says, "lyla, I'm excited that you are here for your check-up today." She asks lyla to sit in the big chair. The chair starts to move back almost becoming flat like a bed!

Dr. Sugarbaum is sitting in one of the small chairs. lyla looks up at the dentist and sees that she is wearing a pink mask, pink gloves and has special glasses on; those are called dental loupes.

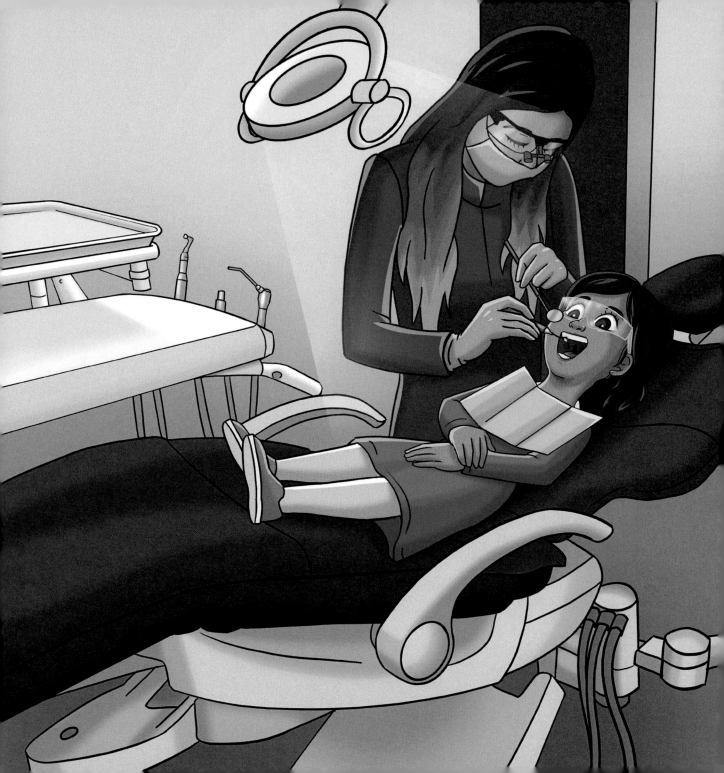

Dr. Sugarbaum says, "open wide" as she begins to count and check lyla's teeth with her special tools: a mirror and an explorer.

Dr. Sugarbaum checks every surface of lyla's teeth and counts aloud, 1, 2, 3, 4, 5, 6, 7, 8, 9, 10. lyla has ten teeth up top and ten teeth on the bottom!

With her explorer, Dr. Sugarbaum touches each of the grooves of lyla's teeth making sure nothing is soft or sticky.

There are a lot of neat things in the operatory. There is a large shiny light above Iyla's head, special eye glasses that protect her eyes and a blue bib so her clothes don't get dirty.

There is a very neat air water syringe that shoots out water and helps wash all of the teeth and also a small little suction tube that sluuurrrrps up all the water in Iyla's mouth.

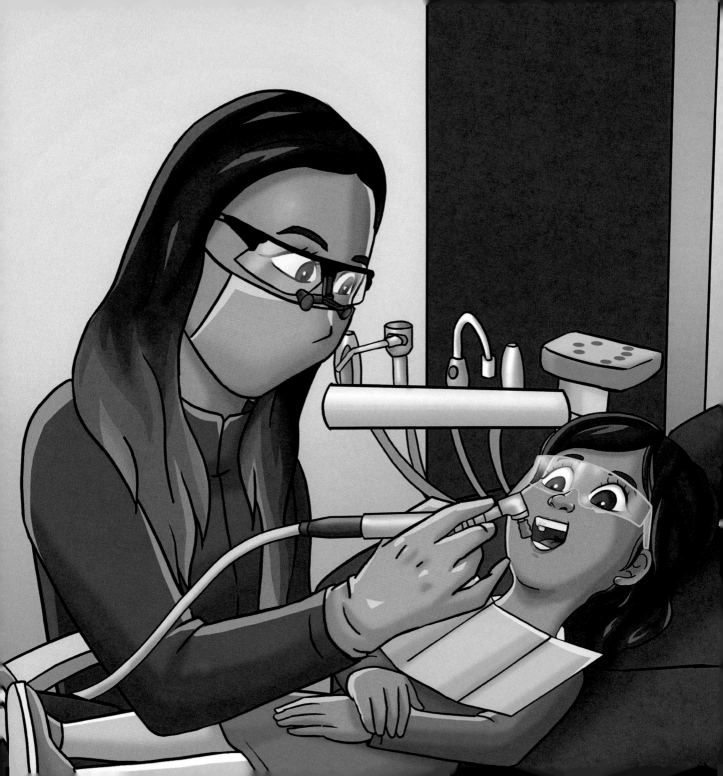

The dentist cleans lyla's teeth one by one and then uses a special paste to polish them! The polish is done with a tool that buzzes loud and feels like it's tickling the teeth.

lyla is surprised, it makes her giggle. "Everything tastes so yummy," says lyla.

Now for the last step, Dr. Sugarbaum paints on a special fluoride varnish on the grooves of the teeth. "This helps to keep the teeth nice and strong," she tells Iyla.

"No cavities! You were a wonderful helper today," says Dr. Sugarbaum, and she tells Iyla to make sure she brushes her teeth twice a day and uses floss at home as well.

lyla jumps out of the chair and heads to a toy chest to pick out a prize.
"Going to the dentist was a lot of fun!" says lyla. She can't wait to go back!

Manufactured by Amazon.ca
Bolton, ON

22299042R00017